JER Juhlin
Juhlin, Emeli,
This is Ms. Marvel /
$4.99   on1203135798

THIS IS MS. MARVEL

Adapted by **Emeli Juhlin**
Illustrated by **Devin Taylor and Vita Efremova**
Based on the Marvel comic book character **Ms. Marvel**

Los Angeles
New York

© 2021 MARVEL

All rights reserved. Published by Marvel Press, an imprint of Buena Vista Books, Inc.
No part of this book may be reproduced or transmitted in any form or by any means,
electronic or mechanical, including photocopying, recording, or by any information
storage and retrieval system, without written permission from the publisher. For
information address Marvel Press, 77 West 66th Street, New York, NY 10023

Printed in the United States of America
First Edition, July 2021 10 9 8 7 6 5 4 3 2 1
Library of Congress Control Number: 2021930706
FAC-029261-21148
ISBN: 978-1-368-07048-5

If you purchased this book without a cover, you should be aware that this book is stolen
property. It was reported as "unsold and destroyed" to the publisher, and neither the
author nor the publisher has received any payment for this "stripped" book.

This is Kamala Khan.

Kamala lives in Jersey City.

She lives with her parents
and brother.

She has great friends.

Kamala is Muslim.

She is a good student.

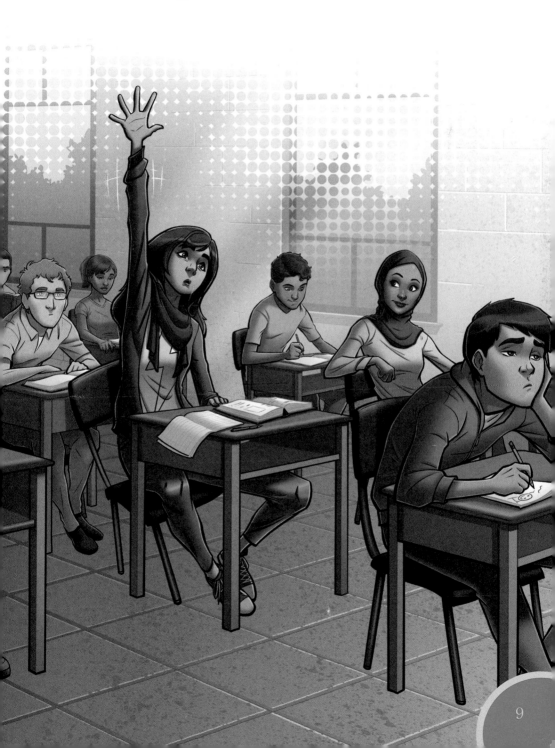

She writes stories about
super heroes.
She likes Captain Marvel
the best.

One night, a strange fog rolls
into the city.

The fog gives Kamala
super-powers!
She can change how she looks.

Kamala makes her own outfit.
She becomes Ms. Marvel.

Ms. Marvel can grow big
or small.
She can stretch parts of her
body.

She has super-speed.

She has super-strength.

She can heal herself.
But it makes her very tired
and hungry.

Ms. Marvel keeps Jersey City
safe.

Sometimes the city is quiet.

Sometimes it needs her help.

Ms. Marvel has to stop the
Inventor!

Captain Marvel will help her.

They work together.

They find where the Inventor
is hiding.

Ms. Marvel grows bigger and bigger!
She is ready.

The Inventor is no match for
Ms. Marvel.

Captain Marvel thanks
Ms. Marvel for her hard work.

Ms. Marvel learns a lot from other heroes.
She is proud to be part of a team.

Jersey City needs a hero.
They need her.

Harris County Public Library, Houston, TX

Kamala Khan is Ms. Marvel!